# I Can Go

**by Anne Giulieri**
illustrated by Mélanie Florian

Look at me.

I can go to the shops.

ORANGES

OPEN

Look at me.

I can go to the park.

5

Look at me.

I can go to the pool.

Look at me.

I can go to the party.

11

Look at me.

I can go to the library.

Look at me.

I can go to the beach.

15

Look at me.

I am at the circus.